The Little Red Hen

A Red Fox Book

Published by Random House Children's Books
61-63 Uxbridge Road, London W5 5SA

A division of The Random House Group Ltd
London Melbourne Sydney Auckland
Johannesburg and agencies throughout the world

7 9 10 8 6

First published in Great Britain by Andersen Press Ltd 1999

Red Fox edition 2000

Printed in Singapore

THE RANDOM HOUSE GROUP Limited Reg. No. 954009
www.kidsatrandomhouse.co.uk

ISBN 9781849411165

The Little Red Hen

retold and illustrated by
Michael Foreman

RED FOX

Down the road and over the hills
lived a little red hen. She lived in
a farmyard with the farm dog,
the farm cat and a big fat pig.
"Oink, oink!"

One day, when the little red hen was out
walking, she found some grains of wheat.
She gathered them up and carried them
back to the farmyard.

"Who will help me plant this wheat?"
she asked.

"Not I," said the dog.
"Not I," said the cat.
"Not I," said the big fat pig.
"Oink, oink!"

"Then I shall do it myself,"
clucked the little red hen.

And she did.

The little red hen cared for the wheat
until it grew tall and golden.
"Who will help me cut the wheat?"
she asked.

"Not I," said the dog.
"Not I," said the cat.
"Not I," said the big fat pig.
"Oink, oink!"

"Then I shall do it myself,"
clucked the little red hen.
And she did.

"Now who will help me carry this wheat to the mill, to be ground into flour?" asked the little red hen.

"Not I," said the dog.
"Not I," said the cat.
"Not I," said the big fat pig.
"Oink, oink!"

"Then I shall do it myself,"
said the little red hen.
And she did.

The miller ground the wheat into flour and put it in a sack, and the little red hen dragged the sack back to the farmyard.

"Who will help me carry this flour
to the baker, to be baked into bread?"
asked the little red hen.

"Not I," said the dog.
"Not I," said the cat.
"You carried it here all right, so you can carry it to the baker," said the big fat pig.
"Oink, oink!"

"And so I shall,"
clucked the little red hen.
And she did.

The baker made the flour into
a wonderful big loaf that smelled of
sunshine and poppies and the little red hen
carried it back to the farmyard.
"Who will help me eat this bread?"
she asked.

"I will!" said the dog.
"I will!" said the cat.
"I will!" said the big fat pig.
"Oink, oink!"

"Oh no, you will not!" clucked the little red hen.
"I have some *new* friends coming for tea!"

And she did!

Oink, oink!

Other books by Michael Foreman:

Cat in the Manger

Dad, I Can't Sleep

Dinosaur Time

Grandfather's Pencil and the Room of Stories

The Little Reindeer

Rock-a-Doodle-Do!

Saving Sinbad

Wonder Goal